Happy Thanksgiving

For the children of Tamaques School,
Westfield, New Jersey
—M. M.

ALADDIN PAPERBACKS
An imprint of Simon & Schuster Children's Publishing Division
1230 Avenue of the Americas, New York, NY 10020
Text copyright © 2005 by Brenda Bowen
Illustrations copyright © 2005 by Mike Gordon
All rights reserved, including the right of reproduction in whole or in part in any form.
READY-TO-READ is a registered trademark of Simon & Schuster, Inc.
ALADDIN PAPERBACKS and colophon are trademarks
of Simon & Schuster, Inc.
Designed by Sammy Yuen Jr.
The text of this book was set in CentSchbook BT.
Manufactured in the United States of America
First Aladdin Paperbacks edition October 2005
2 4 6 8 10 9 7 5 3 1
Library of Congress Cataloging-in-Publication Data
McNamara, Margaret.
Happy Thanksgiving / Margaret McNamara ; illustrated by Mike Gordon.—1st Aladdin
paperback ed.
p. cm.—(Ready-to-read) (Robin Hill School)
Summary: Just as Mrs. Connor's first-grade class finishes dressing up in their
Thanksgiving costumes, a fire drill is called.
ISBN-13: 978-1-4169-0505-9 (Aladdin pbk.)
ISBN-10: 1-4169-0505-7 (Aladdin pbk.)
ISBN-13: 978-1-4169-0506-6 (lib. bdg.)
ISBN-10: 1-4169-0506-5 (lib. bdg.)
[1. Thanksgiving Day—Fiction. 2. Schools—Fiction. 3. Fire drills—Fiction.]
I. Gordon, Mike, ill. II. Title. III. Series.
PZ7.M47879343Hap 2005 [E]—dc22 2004024660

Robin Hill School

Happy Thanksgiving

Written by Margaret McNamara
Illustrated by Mike Gordon

Ready-to-Read
Aladdin Paperbacks
New York London Toronto Sydney

Thanksgiving was coming.
The first graders at
Robin Hill School
were making their costumes.

"Gobble gobble!"
said Griffin.
"That is the sound
turkeys make."

"They make that sound
in the woods,"
said Mrs. Connor.

"Gobble!" Griffin shouted.
"But we are indoors,"
said Mrs. Connor.
"So use your indoor voice."

"Gobble,"
Griffin whispered.

"Put your costumes on,
class," said Mrs. Connor.

"I am a pilgrim!" said Nia.

"I am an American Indian!"
said Becky.

"I am a turkey,"
said Griffin.
"I mean, I am in my
turkey costume."

They were all dressed.
It looked like
the first Thanksgiving.

Then the fire bell rang.

"Fire drill,"
said Mrs. Connor.
The fire bell was noisy.

The fire bell was scary.
But the first graders
knew what to do.

They lined up
at the classroom door.

They followed Mrs. Connor
into the hall,

and outside the school.
No one spoke a word.

Not even Griffin.

The bell rang again.
"That was
the all-clear bell,"
said Mrs. Connor.

"The fire drill is over.
Good job!"

"Look!"
The kindergarten kids
stared at
the first graders.

"They think we
are real pilgrims!"
said Hannah.

"And real Indians!"
said Megan.
"And real turkeys!"
said Griffin.

"Griffin,"
said Mrs. Connor,
"now you may use
your outdoor voice."

"Gobble gobble!"
said Griffin.

"Gobble gobble gobble,"
said the kindergarten kids.

Mrs. Connor smiled.
"Happy Thanksgiving
to you all!"